Publisher's Cataloging-in-Publication
(Provided by Quality Books, Inc.)

Messinger, Robert.
  Why me? : why did I have to get diabetes? / by Robert
Messinger and Laura Messinger.
  p. cm.
  SUMMARY: An unlikely interaction between two
third-grade classmates helps them both come to terms
with the feelings they have about their diabetes.
  Audience: Ages 3-11.
  LCCN 2004094773
  ISBN 1-89323-702-8

  1. Diabetes--Juvenile fiction. 2. Diabetes in
children--Juvenile fiction. [1. Diabetes--Fiction.
2. Diseases--Fiction.] I. Messinger, Laura. II. Title.

PZ7.M5556Why 2004   [E]
                 QBI04-700282

Why Me?

Why Did I Have To Get Diabetes?

by Robert Messinger and Laura Messinger

With special thanks to Owen, Monica, Kira, Mia and Maxx Messinger for their help and support.

SNOOD™ is a registered trademark of David Dobson (www.snood.com),
Rufus and Ruby, the bears with diabetes, are the creation of Carol Cramer, who owns the copyright to Rufus.

Introduction

Hi. My name is Laura. I am nine years old, and I am in third grade.

When I was just three and still in pre-school, I got sick and had to go to the hospital. This wasn't fun for a lot of reasons, mostly because it happened just a few days before Christmas. Anyway, my doctors told me that I have a condition called diabetes (you'll find out later in this book why I call it a condition instead of a disease). Diabetes happens when a part of your body called the pancreas stops making something called insulin, which helps our bodies use the food that we eat. Obviously, insulin is very important!

The only way for my body to get the insulin it needs is for me to take three or four shots a day. And to figure out how much insulin goes into each shot, I have to prick my finger for a blood test six or seven times a day.

I also have to be careful about the foods I eat. Foods like candy, cakes and chips put too much sugar in my blood and work against the insulin shots. My mom and dad and the school nurse write down everything I eat, and then they figure out how much insulin to give me.

Obviously, it isn't a whole lot of fun to take all these shots and blood tests and watch everything you eat, but you kind of get used to it. Besides, I want to stay healthy and do all of the great things I do with my family and friends.

The thing about diabetes is that it's a chronic condition. (The word "chronic" sounds like "kron-ik"). That means it never goes away like a cold or the chicken pox do. So, even though I think I do a pretty good job of living with diabetes, every now and then I still get sad and ask my mom or dad, "Why me? Why did I have to get diabetes?"

My parents tell me that I am doing a great job with my diabetes, and that it's okay to feel sad once in awhile. My dad suggested that he and I sit down together to write a book about how I sometimes feel, to help me understand my feelings a little better. This is our book. I hope you enjoy it.

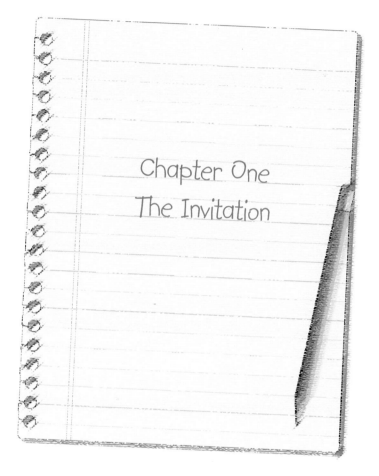

Chapter One

The Invitation

My parents had just received an invitation to Cousin Jennifer's wedding! I don't think I'd been this excited since Christmas!

Now I don't really know Cousin Jennifer all that well. In fact, I'm not sure I'd even be able to pick her out at one of Uncle Maxx's family barbecues. And no kids were going to be invited to the wedding, except Cousin Kira, who was going to be a bridesmaid or something.

So why in the world was I so excited, you ask?

Because I come from a really, really big family with lots and lots of cousins who are kids, too. And since no kids were allowed at the wedding, all the cousins had to go *somewhere*!

Uncle Maxx had arranged for all the kid cousins to come to his house for a huge party. This was going to be like the event of the year for me, because I hardly ever get to see all my cousins at once. We live worlds apart (Mom, Dad and I

live in New Jersey, and most of my cousins live in Pennsylvania). I was looking forward to this party so much I could hardly keep my mind on my school work...or even on my favorite TV shows!

My Cousin Nicole (she's not one of the kid cousins) was going to be in charge of the party. Nicole had taken care of me before, so she knew how to help me take care of my diabetes. This is very important. Anyone who takes care of me has to know how to take my blood test, how to read the results, how to treat my sugar lows, how to give me insulin shots, and what to do in an emergency.

I'm pretty good about helping take care of my diabetes. I've been taking my own blood tests since I was four, and I'm pretty good at feeling when my blood sugar drops too low. But I still need an adult to tell me what to eat and, of course, to give me my insulin shots. So it was important for Cousin Nicole to be at the party.

Nothing could stop this from being the greatest party ever! At least that's what I thought.

Daddy found out just two days before the wedding that Nicole wasn't going to be able to be in charge of the kid cousins party!

"So what?" I thought. "There'll still be an adult there. It won't make any difference."

But Mommy and Daddy didn't quite see it that way.

"Honey," Dad said to me, "We don't think it's a good idea for you to go to this party now that Nicole won't be there."

I couldn't believe what I was hearing! They had to be kidding!

"You know that when we leave you with anyone, that person has to know how to take care of you."

"But you can show them...just like you showed Cousin Nicole and Aunt Monica," I whined (I admit it...sometimes I whine).

"It's not that simple, Laura," said Mommy. "You don't understand..."

"You think I don't understand anything!" I interrupted loudly. This brought the "look" from Dad, and I immediately knew that I had gone too far, and I changed my tone of voice.

"This really makes me sad. I hardly ever get to see my cousins. Please don't get mad, but sometimes I think it's *you* who doesn't understand."

A few seconds passed. Then I said with a very sad voice, "Why me? Why did *I* have to get diabetes?"

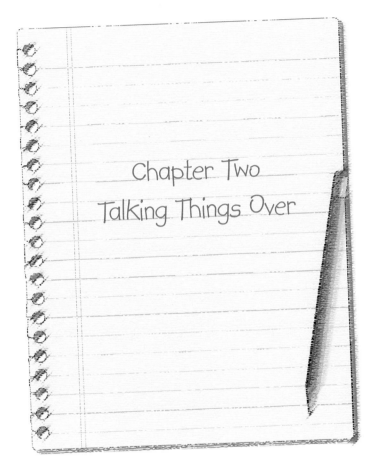

Chapter Two
Talking Things Over

I went to my room to play a game on the computer. Whenever I get sad, I play a game called Snood to take my mind off of things. But this time, I just couldn't keep my mind on the game. After a while, Dad came in.

"How do you feel?" he asked me.

"I'm okay," I said in a low voice, like I really didn't want to be bothered. "I don't feel like I have a sugar low or anything."

"That's not what I mean," said Dad.

I was confused. Grown-ups are always asking me how I feel because of my diabetes. They usually want to know if I'm feeling dizzy or cranky or quiet because of a sugar low or a sugar high. What did Dad mean this time? What did he want to know?

"When Mom and I ask you how you feel, we don't always mean physically. We also want to know how you feel up here." He pointed to my head.

"Oh," I said.

"You've already told us that you're feeling sad because you have to miss the party," said Dad. How else do you feel?"

I got a little annoyed.

"It's not just the party," I snapped. "I *told* you you don't understand!"

"Well, then, help me understand," he replied.

I wasn't really sure what to say. It wasn't always easy to talk about this. I usually never have a hard time speaking my mind, but how I felt about this whole diabetes thing was confusing and difficult to talk about.

"Are you angry at me and Mom?" Dad asked.

"I'm not angry at *you*," I shot back. "I'm angry at those stupid doctors!"

"Because they said you have diabetes?" asked Dad.

"No," I barked. "Because they're supposed to be so smart, but they can't come up with a cure for this stupid thing!"

I couldn't believe I blurted that out! It was something I'd think about sometimes, but I never told it to anyone. Suddenly, I got a lot braver.

"And I guess I *do* get angry at you and Mom sometimes, and sometimes my teachers, too, because none of you understands what it's like to have diabetes!"

Whoops! Did I just go too far? As long as I can remember, I've wanted to make my parents proud of the way I've handled my diabetes. Now I've let them see that maybe I'm not at brave as I've let on.

"I'm only nine, you know," I said in my defense. I wasn't sure just why I said that, but it somehow seemed appropriate.

"I'm sure that even grown-ups who have chronic diseases get angry sometimes," said Dad.

"DADDY!" I interrupted. He knew why.

"I'm sorry. Most adults who have chronic *conditions* feel angry, too."

Dad knew that I didn't like to call my diabetes a disease. When kids hear that you have a "disease," they sometimes get worried that they can catch it, and they stay away from you. It's really frustrating to be known as the kid with the "disease," so we decided to always call it a "condition."

"Anyway," he continued, "it's okay to get angry. And it's normal. The fact that you get angry doesn't take away from the fact that you're handling your diabetes really well, and we're very proud of you."

I jumped out of my chair onto Daddy's lap. What

a relief that he didn't think any less of me for feeling they way I did. Then I looked up and saw Mommy standing in the doorway. She was smiling, but she also had a few tears in her eyes.

"We're both so proud of you," she said as she came in and sat down on my bed. She picked up Ruby, my bear with diabetes. Mom and Dad had given me Ruby a little after I was diagnosed. Ruby has patches where she gets her shots and tests her blood. I guess they gave her to me to help me learn about taking care of diabetes, but I liked her most of all because I could talk to her about how I felt. I always imagined that Ruby understood. (Want to know a secret? I still hug Ruby sometimes at night when I'm feeling a little sad).

"I remember the day the doctor told us you had diabetes," Mom said as she looked at Ruby.

"So do I," I replied. "You cried when the doctor told you."

"You remember that?" Mom asked.

"It made me scared," I said.

"Well, I'm really sorry about that, honey," said Mom. "But you know something? We were scared, too. We didn't really know too much about diabetes or how we were going to learn to take care of you. But they taught us everything we needed to know at the hospital. And after that, we joined special groups of parents whose children also had diabetes, and we learned that we could take care of you and that we could keep your diabetes under control. And that you could have a pretty normal life."

"Do you still get scared?" I asked.

Mom and Dad just looked at each other. I don't think they knew quite what to say, so I said something.

"Even though my diabetes is under control, I still get scared sometimes," I admitted. "I know that it can get really bad if you don't take care of it, and I want to grow up and be a teenager and go to college and have my own family and..."

"You *will* do all those things," Daddy interrupted. "To answer your question, we may still get a little worried sometimes. That's just natural when you're dealing with any condition that doesn't have a cure. But we know we're doing everything we can to keep your condition under control, and we have every confidence that you'll do the same to take care of yourself as you grow up."

Daddy looked over at the computer.

"Hey, I caught you in the middle of a game of Snood! Want some help?"

"Yeah! Let's finish it together! I bet we can still break 100,000 points!" I exclaimed.

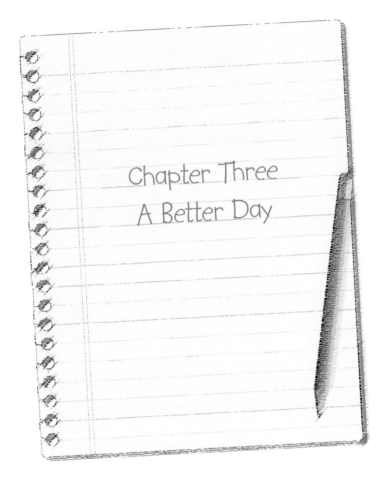

Chapter Three
A Better Day

The next day, I woke up bright and early... even before the alarm clock went off. It still bothered me that I was going to miss the party, but I didn't feel quite as badly as I did the night before. The sun was bright, the birds were chirping, the air was super fresh, and I just had a feeling that it was going to be a great day!

Mom usually has to prod me to get ready in the morning (like Daddy, I'm not really a morning person). But without being reminded, I brushed my teeth, got dressed, brushed my hair, packed my school bag and took my morning blood test. I usually watch TV while Mom makes my breakfast and prepares my insulin shots (I get two shots in the morning…one that works right away, and one that works throughout the day), but that day I felt like taking a walk. So instead of turning on the TV, I attached Dexter's leash to his collar (obviously, he's my dog), and out the door I skipped.

When I got to the corner, I stopped and waited for a blue minivan to pass. Inside the minivan, I recognized Tyler Johnson, a kid from my third grade class.

I wasn't friendly with Tyler. He didn't like playing with girls very much, and he liked to tease us.

He even teased me about my diabetes once in awhile. I couldn't help noticing that he looked pretty sad in that minivan.

"How can anyone be sad on such a lovely day?" I said to Dexter.

I wondered why his parents were driving him to school that day. Tyler always took the bus, and he always sat in the very back seat with his noisy friends. Come to think of it, I hadn't seen Tyler on the bus for about a week, and I don't remember seeing him in class, either.

Anyway, I had better things to think about that day. I started thinking about my ballet recital, which was just a few weeks away, and I also thought about a new book I'd just started reading. Today was *not* going to be a day of sadness for me! I didn't give Tyler Johnson another thought... at least not right away.

At 11:30 every morning, I go to the school nurse to take a blood test. This morning wasn't any different, except for one thing... Tyler Johnson was sitting there in the nurse's office, looking just as glum as he did earlier that morning. He sure didn't look too happy to see me. Instead of going in, I stopped and just stood there for a minute. Then the nurse waved me in and asked me to close the door behind me.

"Hi, Laura," said Mrs. Jones, the school nurse. Mrs. Jones and I are just about as friendly as a kid and a grown-up can be. Besides taking great care of me at school and on field trips, I can tell she really likes me. We laugh a lot, and sometimes she lets me eat lunch with her in her office after I take my 11:30 blood test.

"Laura," said Mrs. Jones, "Tyler has a bit of a secret that he doesn't want any of the children to know just yet. But I think I've convinced him that his secret would be safe with you."

What in the world could this be about? Why would Tyler want to tell me a secret? And why on earth would Mrs. Jones think I'd even *want* to know any of *his* secrets? Uggh!

I didn't know what to say. Mrs. Jones could see that I wasn't very comfortable, and I could see that Tyler was pretty uneasy himself.

"Laura, this is important," said Mrs. Jones. "I trust you, and I know Tyler will learn to trust you, too." I couldn't let Mrs. Jones down. I nodded my head OK.

"Tyler, may I tell Laura what we've been talking about?" asked Mrs. Jones.

Tyler turned his head away from me, and he simply said, "I guess."

"Laura," said Mrs. Jones, "Tyler has been in the hospital for the past week. He's been diagnosed with Type 1 diabetes."

Tyler Johnson has diabetes? I'm ashamed to say it, but my first thought was that it served him right for all the times he teased me about my diabetes. But I remembered what a difficult time I had when I found out about my own diabetes. And I remembered how sad I was just the night before when I learned that I had to miss the kid cousins party because of my diabetes.

"Oh, Tyler, I'm so sorry to hear that," I said. I

was a little surprised at my own comforting words, but after all, no one *deserves* to be sick.

"Yeah, sure you are," replied Tyler sarcastically.

"Laura," said Mrs. Jones, "I've already taken Tyler's lunchtime blood test and given him his shot. I have a few things to do, so I'm going to leave you two alone for a few minutes. I want you to show him how you take your own blood test and then figure out how much insulin I have to give you before lunch."

Mrs. Jones walked out of the office and left me alone with Tyler. After a few uneasy seconds, Tyler spoke.

"You better not tell anyone! Or else!"

"I won't if you don't want me to," I said. "And stop threatening me!"

I took my blood test kit out of the cabinet and prepared for my finger prick. Tyler watched me.

"This is my own fault," Tyler said. "It's because I'm always eating candy when I'm not supposed to. It's my own fault I got diabetes."

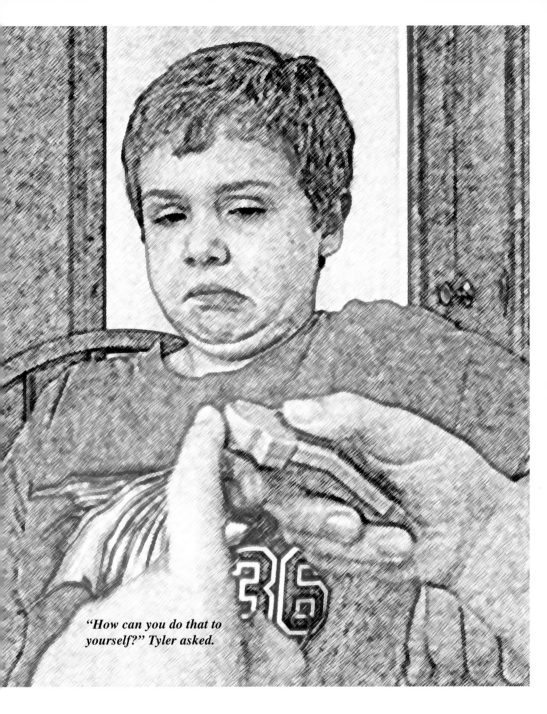

"How can you do that to yourself?" Tyler asked.

"It's *not* your fault," I told him. "It's no one's fault. You probably had a virus or something that made your pancreas stop making insulin. Eating too much candy had nothing to do with it."

I pricked my finger without even flinching and squeezed a drop of blood onto the strip that tests my sugar levels. The blood testing machine started counting down.

"How can you *do* that to yourself?" Tyler asked. He made a face.

"I hardly even feel it anymore," I told him. "You'll be doing it yourself before you know it. I still can't give myself my own shots, though."

We both watched the machine count down.

"Maybe I got diabetes because I don't listen to my parents and because I always get in trouble at school. Maybe it's because I pick on kids...or maybe because I make fun of *your* diabetes. That's probably what happened. I'm being punished."

"It wouldn't hurt for you to start being nicer," I said, "but you didn't get diabetes because you were bad. People just get sick sometimes."

I could tell that Tyler didn't believe a word I was saying. The blood test machine finished counting down and showed that my blood sugar level was 252, which was a little on the high side. I wrote the number on my chart, then I picked up the little book that shows how many grams of carbohydrates are in the food I eat. Tyler looked a little baffled, so I explained what I was doing.

"Most foods contain carbohydrates," I explained. "I call them carbs. Diabetics have to keep track of the carbs we eat because carbs turn into sugar in our bodies. I'm looking up what I'm going to eat for lunch, then I'm going to write down the number of carbs and figure out how much insulin I need."

"I'll never be able to do that," said Tyler.

"I didn't think I'd be able to do it, either," I assured him. "But you will. Besides, you don't have to worry about any of that now. Your parents and Mrs. Jones know how to take care of you. I still can't do it all on my own."

I figured out that my grilled cheese sandwich and milk would contain 57 grams of carbs. Then I looked at my special chart and figured out that I'd need three units of insulin for my lunch and an extra half unit because my sugar number was a little high.

"Why don't you want anyone else to know about your diabetes?" I asked Tyler as I wrote down all the numbers.

"Because they'll know I'm a freak!" he said.

"Well *I'm* not a freak because I have diabetes!" I shot back at him, my feelings more than a little hurt.

Mrs. Jones had just come back into the office and heard what was said.

"Nobody here is a freak," she responded. "People aren't going to judge you by your condition. It's not your diabetes that makes you who you are. It's how you act and what you do that makes you who you are."

Mrs. Jones told Tyler to go back to class and get ready for lunch. After he left, she looked at the number on my blood test machine and at the carb and insulin amounts I'd written down. (Even though I do a lot to help take care of myself, grown-ups still double check everything...after all, I *am* only nine).

As Mrs. Jones prepared my insulin shot, she said, "I'm sorry if Tyler hurt your feelings."

"That's OK," I replied, even though I still thought he was being mean.

"I know that the two of you don't always get along, and I think it's really very nice of you help him out," said Mrs. Jones.

Mrs. Jones always seems to know what to say to make me feel better.

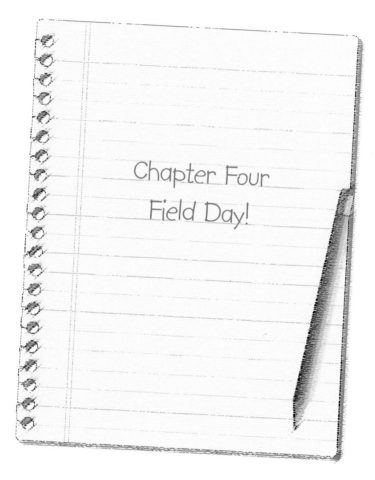

Chapter Four
Field Day!

Tyler and I didn't talk too much over the next few days. In fact, it seemed like he did his best to avoid me. He asked Mrs. Jones if he could go for his blood tests and shots after I'd go for mine, and she told him that was okay if that's what he really wanted to do. Also, he didn't seem to be spending as much time with his regular friends, and he was spending most of recess by himself on the monkey bars. In a way, it was refreshing that he wasn't bothering anyone. But on the other hand, I knew he was sad, and that made me a little sad, too. But I figured there was nothing I could do to help him if he didn't want my help. Besides, I wasn't really sure what help I could give him even if he wanted it.

Things stayed pretty much the same over the next few weeks. The kid cousins party came and went. I was still sad that I couldn't go, but Mom and Dad took me to a movie that day to keep my mind off of it.

Besides, Field Day was coming soon, and I was really looking forward to it! Last year, I was the fastest runner in my class. I'd made it to the finals in the 50-yard dash, but I lost the second grade title to Maria Campbell from Ms. Meyerson's class. I was looking forward to a rematch!

The races started about 9:30 on Field Day. The first round is set up so two kids run 50 yards at the same time until everyone has run. The kid with the fastest overall time moves on to the finals. Mrs. Mendez, the gym teacher, called my name, and I moved to the starting line. Then she called the kid who was going to run next to me... *Tyler Johnson.* I don't know why this bothered me, but it did. This was the closest contact we'd had since the nurse's office, and it made me feel a bit uncomfortable.

Tyler came to the line and stood next to me. I glanced over at him, but I didn't say anything because it seemed like he was avoiding looking at me. Besides, I had to concentrate on the race.

The whistle blew, and we both took off as fast as we could. Tyler got off to a good start ahead of me, and I really had to pour it on. But then, all of a sudden, he just stopped. I saw the look on his face, and I knew what was happening. I stopped dead in my tracks.

"I don't feel too good," Tyler said to me. He looked frightened. "What's happening to me?"

"I think you're having a sugar low, Tyler," I said. "It happens when the insulin makes your blood sugar go too low. You'll be okay after you have some juice and a snack."

Mrs. Mendez came over right away and told Tyler to go to the nurse's office.

"I'll go with him," I volunteered.

Mrs. Jones took Tyler's blood test. It was 63, which is low enough to make you feel dizzy or confused. It turned out that this was the first time that Tyler had ever felt a sugar low.

"It's okay, Tyler," Mrs. Jones assured him. "You'll be fine about 15 minutes after you drink this juice and have these crackers."

"That's just what I told him," I said.

"Laura, do you want to stay with Tyler until he's feeling better?" asked Mrs. Jones.

I looked at Tyler. He didn't have anything to say,

but he didn't seem to object, either.

"Sure," I told Mrs. Jones. "I'll stay."

In about five minutes, the color seemed to be coming back to Tyler's face. A few minutes after that, he started talking.

"Does this happen to you a lot?" he asked me.

"Not as much as it used to, but yeah, it does happen," I replied. "My doctor says it's important that I can recognize my lows so I can fix them fast."

"This really stinks," he said. "I hate it!"

"So do I," I replied.

Tyler seemed surprised at my response. How could he think even for a minute that I wouldn't hate having diabetes!

"Of course I hate it," I said to him. "Diabetes isn't fun."

"But you're always so happy and you're always playing and raising your hand in class and everything. On your birthday, you even brought cup cakes in for the whole class, even though you couldn't have one, and you were still happy."

"I was happy because it was my birthday and because I was celebrating it with my friends. I *hate* that everyone else can have cup cakes and I can't. But it made my friends happy, and that made me happy."

Tyler looked confused.

"Look," I explained, "it's not fun missing out on some things. I *hate* when I have to stop having fun or miss class when I have a sugar low and have to go to the nurse. I *hate* when sometimes I have to stay in at recess to make up the work I missed. It *is* unfair. I still cry and feel angry and ask, 'Why me?'"

I could tell that Tyler didn't believe me, so I told him all about the cousins party I had to miss because there was no one to watch out for me and all the whining I did over it and how Mom and Dad tried to make me feel better. Going over the whole thing again wasn't fun, and I felt a little weird telling all this personal stuff to someone I hardly knew and didn't really like, but somehow it seemed like the right thing to do.

I guess Tyler wasn't sure what to say. He looked like he was deep in thought for what seemed like forever. When he finally did speak, all he said was, "I've gotta go to the bathroom," and he got up and walked into the nurse's lavatory.

Mrs. Jones, who had been sitting there quietly the whole time, spoke up after Tyler shut the door.

"I think he's going to be fine," she said. "It's just going to take some time." Then she looked me straight in the eyes and said, "Laura, what you're doing for Tyler is very nice."

"I just wish *he* were a little nicer," I replied. I hesitated a little, then I added, "I'm not so sure I'm the best person to help him."

"Why not?" asked Mrs. Jones, looking puzzled. "You've been doing so well managing your diabetes."

"Not always," I admitted. "Sometimes, I still try to talk my parents into letting me have more carbs than I'm allowed. And I still can't help it

when I get mad or cranky when I have a low or a high. And what about the way I acted when I learned I couldn't go to the cousins party? And..."

"Whoa, hold on," interrupted Mrs. Jones. "Why are you being so hard on yourself? Is helping Tyler bringing this on?"

"I don't know. Maybe a little. Maybe it's just making me think about stuff a little more."

"Well, talking about how you feel is the most important thing you can do when you're feeling sad or frustrated," she said. "And besides, I think you *are* the best person to help Tyler. You're probably one of the only people in this whole school who can understand what Tyler is actually going through, because you're going through so many of the same things yourself. I think it's important for him to see that. And it's important that he sees how normal you make your life in spite of your condition."

Mrs. Jones paused for a few seconds while I took this all in. Then she added, "And you know, in the long run, maybe Tyler can help you, too."

Tyler help *me*? How in the world could he do *that*? My face probably showed what I was thinking because Mrs. Jones added, "You may not believe that right now, but sometimes the support we need comes from the most unlikely places."

We heard the toilet flush, so we knew that Tyler was about to come out.

"Sure, you may still have some things to work on," Mrs. Jones said. "That's only natural. We all have things we have to work on. But don't you ever downplay all the good things you do for yourself. You're learning piano and acting and ballet. You concentrate on doing well in school. You have a lot of friends."

"What I really admire about you," she said, "is that you focus more on what you *can* do than on what you *can't* do. As long as you never stop doing that, you'll be fine."

Tyler came out of the bathroom looking a whole lot better than he did out on the track field. I think he even had a bit of a smile on his face. Mrs. Jones took his blood test (I left the room while she did this, because I knew it still made Tyler uncomfortable to have someone there), and his sugar level was 119, which is good.

"Okay, you two," she said. "Back to Field Day!"

Tyler and I hurried down the hallway toward the door.

"Why did you do that?" he asked me.

"Huh? Why did I do what?"

"I know how much it meant to you to win that stupid 50-yard dash this year. And now you won't because you stopped to help me."

Ouch! I didn't even think of that! I really *did* want to win that event for our class. I was definitely disappointed. But at the same time, I felt kind of good.

Chapter Five
Tyler Makes a Choice

It really was the perfect spring day for Field Day. The sun was bright, and the trees were completely filled with new green leaves. There was a mild breeze that carried the sweet smell of the newly sprouted flowers throughout the field and the playground. I was feeling great, even if I did have to wait until next year to try to win that 50-yard dash!

The rest of the day's events went as planned. I did have to treat a sugar low between the Softball Toss and the Relay Race, but I didn't even go inside for that. I just sat down on the new grass and drank the juice box I'd brought with me just in case.

Finally, it was time for the last event of the day... the three-legged race. If our class won this event, we'd be ahead in points and be presented with the "United in Sportsmanship" trophy at the next assembly.

The way this event works is that the class selects one person to compete, and then that person chooses his or her partner. There was little doubt whom the class was going to choose this year...

Tyler Johnson! He was really good at the three-legged race. We'd never seen him fall even once during our practice sessions. The only question remained was whom he would choose as his partner. We all assumed it would be Randy Billings or one of his other noisy friends.

The class voted by a show of hands, and Tyler was indeed chosen to compete. I looked over at him, wondering whether or not he was up for it. He looked a little worried as he looked around at the rest of the group.

"Who's your partner going to be, Tyler?" asked Mrs. Mendez.

Tyler looked around for a few more moments, then his eyes stopped directly at me. A few more seconds went by, and he said, "Laura. Laura is going to be my partner."

I'm sure that I heard a bit of a gasp go up from the class. I really am a fast runner, but I'm not particularly known for my coordination! And it takes really good coordination to win a three-legged race! I just stood there, stunned.

Tyler picked up the rope that would tie our legs together and walked over to me.

"We can do this," he said, with a determination I hadn't seen from him in weeks.

His friend Randy came over and said to Tyler, "How can you do this? How can you choose 'diabetes girl' over your friends?"

Tyler turned red, and for a minute I thought he was going to shove Randy. But the whistle blew for everyone to get ready, and we took our positions and tied our legs together.

"The trick is to start together with our inside legs," said Tyler as we positioned our hands around each other's waists. "After that, we'll get into a rhythm. My dad taught me how to do this. Now this part is very important, so listen... *never let go of my waist.*"

I was still nervous as I listened to Tyler's instructions. He must have seen that, and he reassured me, "Don't worry. We can do this."

"You're fast," he said. "Go as fast as you can

and I'll follow. Just remember that we have to start together."

It seemed like we were positioned at the starting line forever waiting for the whistle. In the background, I could hear our class members shouting words of encouragement. Finally, the whistle sounded, and we took off like a bolt of lightning. I was surprised that I was able to start off just as Tyler had instructed and at how easy it was to maintain a rhythm. We got off to an early lead, and it looked like we were sure to win. Then the unthinkable happened! A bee landed right on the hand I had around Tyler's waist. Anyone who knows me can tell you that there's little in the world I'm more frightened of than bees! I panicked, of course. I removed my hand from Tyler's waist and started waving it wildly. It was then that I realized why Tyler said to keep my hand on his waist. Removing it immediately threw us off balance, and our rhythm was lost! I started to go down. It felt like I was falling in slow motion. But Tyler never moved his hand from my waist. He held it there tightly, and he sort of scooped me back up. I instinctively put my hand

Tyler never moved his hand from my waist...he sort of scooped me back up.

back around his waist (thankfully, the bee was gone now), and we regained our balance in a few seconds.

But it was too late, I thought. Heather Blackburn and Todd Winslow had taken the lead during the few seconds of my stumble.

"Let's turn it up, Laura!" Tyler shouted. "We can still do this!"

This was a different Tyler than I'd known for the past few weeks. He was determined to keep trying, even though things didn't look so good right then. His positive attitude, combined with the cheers from our classmates, made me really want to try, too.

"On my count," I shouted. "One-two-three."

And turn it up we did! We both gave it everything we had, together and in rhythm! And we reached the finish line a full two steps ahead of Heather and Todd! We fell to the ground laughing. "That stupid bee!" I joked.

Our classmates surrounded us, cheering. Tyler untied the rope that kept our legs together, and

he handed it to me.

"Keep this as a souvenir," he said.

"No, Tyler," I said, handing it back to him. "You keep it. Keep it as a reminder of what you did here today."

Chapter Six
The Big Surprise

The next three weeks were pretty full. With the school year winding down, we had to finish up a lot of projects and take some extra tests. Plus, there was my ballet recital to practice for. Tyler and I didn't get a chance to talk too much during those few weeks. But I did notice some changes in him. He wasn't keeping to himself as much as he did after he found out about his diabetes. He still hung out with his noisy friends, but he didn't seem to be such a pest anymore. He seemed more willing to be helpful to other kids. And the biggest change I saw was that he'd smile at me and even say hello when we passed each other in the hall on our daily trips to the nurse's office.

I was also pretty busy getting ready for my final Sunday school tests. I guess I stayed up studying a little too late the night before the last day of Sunday school. I just didn't want to get out of bed! Dad kind of rushed me to get ready with a little more zest than usual, which I thought was a little odd, because Dad likes to be a bit lazy on Sunday mornings.

He dropped me off promptly at 10:00, and he told me that he'd pick me up promptly at noon.

Who's he kidding, I wondered. Dad's car was always the last one on the pick-up line at Sunday school.

But 12 o'clock came, and there was Dad's car, first on line. Mom was with him, too, which was strange, because she usually spends the early part of Sunday afternoons in her studio, where she makes jewelry.

"Daddy, what's going on?" I asked as soon as I hopped in the car.

"What do you mean, Sweetie?"

"You *never* pick me up first. And Mom's here instead of in her studio. Are we doing something special today?"

He didn't really answer me. He just talked about what a beautiful day it was, and how happy I must be that summer was finally on its way. But I *knew* something was strange when he didn't make his usual turn to go to his favorite taco place, which is what we do *every* Sunday after he picks me up.

A few minutes later, we turned onto our street.

Our usually peaceful and empty road was jammed with cars parked bumper-to-bumper.

"I guess one of the neighbors is having a big barbecue or something," I said.

We managed to squeeze into our driveway between two of the parked cars, and Dad reached into his pockets for his house keys.

"Darn," he said. "I think I left my keys on the picnic table in the backyard. Can you get them for me?"

"Sure," I told him, and I skipped off to the backyard.

This Sunday morning was getting stranger and stranger. Dad never left the house without his keys. And I could hear Dexter barking in the backyard. We *never* let him out of the house alone.

As I rounded the corner to the backyard, Dexter ran to greet me. I bent down to pick him up.

"Hey, boy, what are you doing out here all by yourself?" I asked him. Before he could bark his answer, I was startled by a chorus of giggles.

I looked up, and to my surprise, my backyard was filled with an army of cousins! Mom and Dad had made a kid cousins party for *me*!

Dad and Mom came up behind me, and Dad asked, "Surprised?"

Was I ever surprised!

"I can't believe you did this for me!" I exclaimed. "You're the best parents in the whole world!"

"We can't take all the credit," Mom said. "In fact, it was *their* idea."

Mom pointed to the far corner of the backyard.

There, among a sea of cousins, stood two very familiar non-cousin figures...Mrs. Jones and *Tyler*.

I made my way over to them, stopping to hug cousins along the way. When I finally got to where they were standing, all I could say was, "Thank you, thank you, thank you!"

"It was really all Tyler's idea," said Mrs. Jones, as Tyler blushed. "He knew how unhappy you were to miss the cousins party in Pennsylvania,

so he suggested that we talk to your parents about bringing your cousins to New Jersey. And your parents thought it was a *wonderful* idea!"

"Tyler," I said, "I could just *hug* you!"

"Don't you *dare!*" was his immediate reply.

"OK, no hug," I said, as I planted a quick kiss on his cheek.

"And no kissing, either!" he responded with a laugh as he wiped my kiss away.

The party turned out to be great fun. We played

games and ate lots of hot dogs all afternoon (of course, Tyler and I had to check our blood and get our shots…and he didn't mind doing either in front of me now). Tyler got along with my cousins really well, and he even swapped email addresses with some of them.

I never would have guessed what a sweet kid Tyler could be. I guess Mrs. Jones was right, that friends can come from the most unlikely of places. Tyler even stayed after all the cousins had left to help us clean up.

Tyler and I spoke as we gathered up the greasy paper plates and half-filled cups.

"What you did for me was really nice, Tyler," I told him.

He deposited a pile of trash into a big plastic garbage bag, and then he reached deep into his pocket. He pulled out something and handed it to me.

"It's the rope you told me to keep…the one that we used in the three-legged race," he said. "Well, it's actually only *half* of the rope. I wanted to

keep half for myself."

I didn't know how to respond. Tyler continued.

"When you said to keep it as a reminder of what I did that day, I thought you meant just the race. But now I know you meant something more... that it should always remind me that I don't have to let my diabetes get in the way of who I am. I may be a kid who has diabetes, but that's not *all* I am."

I was genuinely touched. I took my half of the rope and I held it tightly.

"I'll keep it always and use it to remind me, too," I said.

"I'm not ready to let the other kids know about this yet," commented Tyler. "I don't want to be teased."

"Take your time," I told him. "It's really your business who you tell. There'll always be a few kids who don't understand or who are just mean. But for me, I've found that it's tough to keep secrets from my friends...and that most kids really *are* understanding."

"Well, maybe after summer vacation..."

"I'm not trying to push you to do anything," I interrupted. "I'm just telling you what works for me. Just so you know."

"You know what helps me a lot?" I asked Tyler as I picked up a really gooey napkin.

"What?" he asked.

"Hope. I always keep hoping that they'll find a cure someday. And I ask my mom and dad to always read me stories about what the doctors are doing to find a cure. They really are doing a lot."

"Hope," said Tyler. "Yeah, I hope they find a cure, too."

As we finished cleaning up the after-party mess, I couldn't help but think about what a lucky girl I am, even though I have diabetes. I have a family that loves me, the greatest friends in the world, things that really interest me, things that I love to do, teachers and care givers who really support what I do, and so much more! I'm sure things will still happen that make me ask, "Why me?" But as long as I have all of these things, and as long as I have hope, I know I'll always have a happy and productive life.

THE END

Resources

Following are resources readers should find helpful in learning to help children cope emotionally and physically with diabetes and other chronic illnesses:

American Diabetes Association (www.diabetes.org)
Especially helpful is the section *For Parents and Kids*, sub-sections *Youth Zone* and *For Teens*.

Children with Diabetes (www.childrenwithdiabetes.com)
This is an online community that includes chat rooms and support groups.

Juvenile Diabetes Research Foundation (www.jdrf.org)
This website features a wealth of information for parents as well as "JDRF Kids Online" with pen pals, children's art and stories about dealing with diabetes on a daily basis.

Kids Health (http://kidshealth.org)
Sections for parents, kids, teens. Especially helpful is the section about dealing with feelings, including an article for kids about chronic illnesses (enter "Chronic Illness" in search box, then click on "When Someone You Know Has a Chronic Illness").

Kim Gosselin, JayJo Books (www.jayjo.com)
Ms. Gosselin's *Taking Diabetes to School* was the first in her widely acclaimed "The Special Kids in School" series, which provides insightful tools to help children develop an understanding of their chronic illnesses and help them build self-esteem.

National Library of Medicine and National Institutes of Health (www.nlm.nih.gov/medlineplus/juvenilediabetes.html)
A lot to type in, but well worth it. This site provides a wide assortment of information links, including articles on coping with chronic illness from the American Diabetes Association and American College of Physicians.